For Ethan —T.R.

randomhousekids.com

ISBN 978-0-7364-3636-6 (trade)
ISBN 978-0-7364-8229-5 (lib. bdg.)

Printed in the United States of America

10 9 8 7 6 5 4 3 2 1

The Great Mountain Adventure

By Tennant Redbank

Illustrated by Michela Frare and Angela Capolupo

Random House 🏠 New York

"Last one to the top is a pampered pet!" Sultan called. He raced to one ladder on the jungle gym and started climbing.

Sultan liked to be first . . . and fastest. Luckily, this was his home turf, the Jungly Jungle Gym in Whisker Haven. He knew it as well as he knew the stripes on his tiger tail.

He scrambled to the top. *Victory!*

His friend Treasure joined him a moment later. "Ooh," she said, out of breath. "What a great race!"

Dreamy, the pink kitten, yawned. Sultan, Berry, Treasure, Petite, and Pumpkin had all been running around at top speed. But Dreamy? She hadn't moved from her perch at the top of the Jungly Jungle Gym.

"Just watching all that running and climbing makes me sleepy," she said.

Sultan shook his head. Everything made Dreamy sleepy. He had never felt like that. He loved to run! And jump! And move, move, move!

Sultan rolled on his back and swished his tail. There was nothing he loved more than playing on his jungle gym with his friends. Well, almost nothing.

He popped back to his paws and scanned the area. Where was it? Where . . . ?

He relaxed when he spotted his favorite toy—a golden rubber ball, the best ball in the whole world.

"Did I ever tell you how I found my golden ball?" Sultan asked his friends.

"The one in the corner? Near the end

of the slide?" Petite said. She tossed her mane away from her eyes.

Sultan nodded.

"Tell us! Tell us!" the pets cried.

Pumpkin twirled three times, then settled next to Sultan. Berry hopped over. Treasure and Petite gathered around, too. Even Dreamy shifted her napping spot to be closer to her friends.

"It was back in Agrabah," Sultan said, "by Jasmine's palace." Jasmine was Sultan's princess and dearest friend. They'd shared lots of great adventures together—kind of like the adventures he'd had so far in Whisker Haven!

"I'd heard about a treasure cave," Sultan went on. "It was full of gold and jewels and rare coins. If you could sneak something out, you could keep it. But it wasn't easy." The little tiger shook his head. "It was guarded by . . . a snake!"

Berry's eyes widened. "A snake?" she repeated in a hushed voice.

Sultan nodded. "He had scaly red skin and sharp fangs. He was SCARY!"

"You saw him?" Treasure asked.

"I did!" Sultan said. "I crept into

the cave. The snake was asleep by the entrance. I looked around. But I didn't see anything I wanted."

"Not even a ruby-studded kitty bed?" Dreamy asked. "I would want that."

Sultan hid a smile. He knew Dreamy hadn't really been napping. She'd been listening all along!

"Then I spotted it." Sultan dropped his voice to a whisper. "On the other side of the cave was a ball as golden as the sun. I sneaked across the cave. The snake slept on. I climbed a pile of silver coins. But when I reached out my paw and touched the ball, the snake's eyes flew open!"

The pets gasped.

"What did you do?" Petite asked.

"I took the ball and . . ." Sultan paused.

The other pets leaned forward.

"I threw it over the snake's head!" Sultan told them.

"You did WHAT?" Treasure yelped.

"He was so surprised, I was able to dash right past him," Sultan said. "But on my way out, I made sure to snag the ball."

The pets turned to gaze at the golden ball.

"What an adventure!" Treasure said.

"No wonder it means so much to you," Petite added.

"Just as much as my friends!" Sultan jumped to his paws. "Enough sitting! Let's play!" He tore off across the

sand. He leaped to the ground. He dashed
around the back and climbed up to the
slide.

"Race you!" Treasure said, jumping
onto the slide.

Sultan bolted after her and caught up in seconds. The tiger and the kitten tumbled down the slide together. Sultan spat out strands of Treasure's fur. Her fluffy tail covered his eyes.

"I can't see," he said with a laugh. "Are we . . . ?" He felt the slide drop out from under him. They must have reached the bottom! Sultan stuck out his paws to break his fall.

POP!

"Uh-oh," Treasure whispered.

Sultan shook Treasure's tail off his face. The gold rubber ball lay all around him in tatters. He picked up a scrap in his paw.

"My ball?" He looked at Treasure. The other pets stood next to her.

Treasure was still for a moment. Then she nodded.

"My golden ball." Sultan sniffled and blinked back tears.

Pumpkin nuzzled up to comfort him.

"We . . . we'll get another one," Berry said.

"Where?" Sultan asked. "In Agrabah? The snake will be watching this time. I won't be able to surprise him again. There's probably not another ball like this, anyway."

The pets were quiet.

"Maybe not in Agrabah," Berry said. "But what about in Whisker Haven

Village? Let's go to the Squeak and Ball Supply Shop!"

Pumpkin danced a happy dance. "That's right. The Squeak and Ball has tons of great toys!"

Sultan let the scrap of golden rubber drop to the ground. Whisker Haven Village? No way would it have a ball this special. But his friends didn't know that. They were trying to help.

"All right." Sultan tried to sound cheerful. "Let's go."

✳

A gently sloped cobblestone path led the pets from the palace to the village and to a sweet yellow cottage with a backyard surrounded by a brick wall. A sign near the door read THE SQUEAK & BALL SUPPLY SHOP.

"Go on," Berry prompted Sultan.

Just then, the door opened. Sultan heard pawsteps, and a dainty wiener dog in a yellow dress greeted them. It was Lucy, the owner of the shop.

"Come in," Lucy said. "How can I help you?"

"I'm looking for a ball," Sultan told her. "A very special ball. One that is golden like the sun and made by magic."

Lucy tilted her head. "I'm not sure we have a ball exactly like that. But we have lots of others. Please come in and take a look!"

Lucy led the pets inside. The shop was filled with balls and toys of all kinds. Red balls with pink stars, green balls with polka dots, purple balls with tiger stripes. Chewy toys, squeaky toys, rope toys. It was a pet toy extravaganza!

"How about the one with tiger stripes?"

Petite asked, pointing to a nearby shelf.

Sultan bounced the ball halfheartedly. It was nice, but it wasn't right for him.

"Check out this chewy bone!" Pumpkin called.

"Oh, this feather bed is dreamy," Dreamy said, settling into a white kitten bed.

"Are you looking for something that squeaks?" Lucy asked Sultan.

Sultan shook his head. "No, I'd like something *magical*."

"His last ball came from a treasure

cave," Treasure explained. "He had to sneak past a snake to get it. And climb a pile of silver coins. It was an adventure!"

"I see," Lucy said thoughtfully.

"What about this one, Sultan?" Petite asked. She pointed a hoof at a beautiful ball on a shelf in the corner. It was midnight blue with bright blue paw prints. When the light hit it, the paw prints shimmered like magic.

For a moment, Sultan's heart leaped. Then he shook his head. Sure, it was nice. But how could it compare to his golden ball, the ball he'd gotten from a snake's cave? It wasn't the same. Nothing was.

"Maybe I don't have the right ball in the shop," Lucy said. She leaned closer to Sultan. "But I know of a very special ball. Only the brave can find it."

At the word "brave," Sultan's ears pricked up. "I'm brave," he said.

"*Really* brave," Lucy said. "You'll have to climb a mountain, cross the woods, and scale a high wall to get it."

Sultan's tiger heart began to race. Climb a mountain? Cross the woods? Scale a high wall?

"Count me in!" he said.

Lucy went into a back room for a few minutes. When she returned, she pressed a scroll into Sultan's paws. "This map will lead you there," she said. "Are you sure you want to try?"

Sultan nodded. Of course he was sure!

Holding his breath, he unrolled the map. Yes, there was the mountain to climb! There were the woods to cross! There was the wall to scale!

"When do we leave?" Treasure asked.

"You're coming?" Sultan said.

"Of course," Treasure said. "We can't let you have an adventure alone!"

The other pets nodded, even Dreamy.

Sultan's whiskers twitched. "Don't you want to stay here, Dreamy?" he asked.

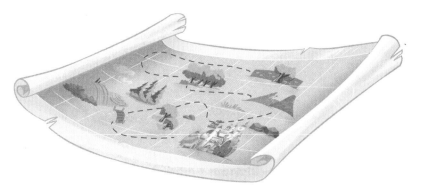

Dreamy could hardly stay awake for an hour at a time!

Dreamy's cat eyes met his. "Finding the ball is your dream," she said. "You may need help."

Sultan was about to object when Petite leaned down and touched noses with the pink kitten. "If you need a nap, you can rest on my back," Petite said.

"Okay," Sultan said. "We're all going!"

Lucy led them to the front door. She pointed up the hill, past the Pawlace. "See the mountain?" she asked. "That's where your adventure begins."

Sultan looked at the mountain. It rose, blue and misty, above the village of Whisker Haven. Dark clouds pooled around the peak. An excited tiger-cub roar rumbled in his throat. This was going to be fun!

Sultan took the lead up the cobblestone path that led out of town. They crossed a field to the base of the mountain. Then the friends started climbing.

Sultan dashed forward to scout out the route. Up ahead, the incline got steeper. The path got rougher. The rocks got larger. He ran back. What was taking so long? His friends were moving *soooo sloooowly.* Maybe he should have come on this adventure alone.

Sultan paced back and forth. Wait! He knew a sure way to get everyone going.

"Last one to the top is a pampered pet!" he shouted.

"Hey!" Pumpkin called. "I like being a pampered pet!"

Sultan grinned and bounded up the mountain. He glanced back. Treasure scrambled right at his heels. Pumpkin and Petite scurried behind her. Even Dreamy had picked up the pace.

Sultan's paw kicked loose a pebble, and it bounced down the path. Petite, below him, ducked out of the way.

"Be careful!" Berry called. "You don't want to start a rock—"

A rumbling above them drowned out the rest of Berry's words. Sultan looked up. It seemed like the mountain was moving.

Petite whinnied a warning. "Rockslide!" she yelled. "Get off the path!"

Sultan leaped to one side. Berry hopped onto the boulder near him. Next to them, Pumpkin's paws skittered on

stone. Sultan pulled her to safety just as a giant boulder and several smaller rocks tumbled past.

On the other side of the path, Petite, Treasure, and Dreamy watched, wide-eyed.

"That was close," Sultan said. He'd wanted to go fast. He'd wanted to be first. Maybe it was more important to be careful.

"Is this an adventure?" Berry asked, her tail twitching. "I'm not sure I like it!"

Sultan leaped to his paws, all doubt gone. "Yes," he said. "Now it's a *real* adventure! Just like in the snake's cave. We just have to cross the peak, and it's on to the woods. Or does the wall come next? I can't remember. . . ." He looked around for the map. He'd had it right before the rockslide.

It wasn't there!

"The rocks!" he cried. "They must have swept the map away!"

"No, they didn't." Dreamy pushed the map toward him with her nose. "I saw it drop when you jumped. So I snatched it up for you."

Dreamy had saved the map? *Phew!* Without the map, they'd be lost! Sultan tilted his head. Maybe there was more to Dreamy than naps.

Sultan looked up the mountain again, and his tail swished. "Come on," he said. "We have a mountain to climb!"

The sun was high overhead when they reached the other side of the mountain. There, rocks and boulders gave way to shrubs and trees. Tall branches blocked out the sky. Green vines hung from them. Lush moss covered the dirt like a carpet.

"The woods," Sultan whispered. He loved a good forest more than any pet.

"No rockslides here," Pumpkin said cheerfully.

"I'll go first!" Sultan said. First and fastest, that was him! But as he bounded forward, he felt a little twinge. What about the rockslide? Was it so important to be first? Maybe he should let someone else lead.

Sultan shook the doubt away. After all, this was *his* adventure!

The path started off clear and wide. Then it began to narrow. Roots poked up through the dirt, and vines hung across the way. Before long, the path was gone. All around were trees and vines.

No path? How could Sultan get to his new ball without a path?

"I'll make a path!" he said.

He slashed at the vines, slicing them with his claws. "This is kind of fun!" he said. "It's an—"

"Adventure!" the other pets shouted together.

Slash! Slash! Slash! Sultan tore through the leaves and branches and tossed them aside. It was exciting to blaze a trail like this! With a growl, he attacked a hairy vine with purple leaves that hung in front of him.

Berry giggled. "Go get 'em, tiger!" she said.

Sultan tore at the vine, but it was stubborn. Instead of falling to the ground, the vine clung to his paws. It tangled

around his tail. It wrapped around his back and belly and started to tighten. Sultan felt his paws lift off the ground.

Hey! They didn't have vines like this in Agrabah!

"Help!" he shouted just before a leaf covered his mouth.

Petite whinnied a warning. "That's no regular vine! That's a strangler fig! I remember reading about them in a book. They're dangerous. Only one thing will make a strangler fig relax. . . ."

"What?" Treasure and Pumpkin asked at the same time.

Petite ducked behind her mane. "I can't remember!" she wailed.

"I'll scare it with my bark!" Pumpkin said. She planted her paws in the dirt

and barked loudly at the vine. But the vine didn't flinch. In fact, the loud noise seemed to make it squeeze tighter!

Sultan had sneaked past a snake. He'd survived a rockslide. Was a plant going to be his last adventure?

But Petite, Berry, Pumpkin, and Treasure didn't give up. They each grabbed one of Sultan's paws and pulled. His friends tugged him in one direction. The vine tugged him in the other.

Then Sultan heard a song, a lullaby. Dreamy was singing!

"That's right!" Petite yelled. "*Singing!* Strangler figs like music!"

Already, the vine felt looser. Sultan looked up. It was stretching, stretching, streeetchiiiiing—

SNAP!

The vine broke!

Sultan tumbled to the ground. He landed in a soft heap with his friends.

"Phew!" Sultan said. He gave Dreamy a grateful nod.

"How did you know to sing?" Petite asked her.

Dreamy shrugged. "It's not my first

time in the woods, you know," she said.

"What an adventure," Treasure said softly.

"Let's get out of here!" Berry said. "And from now on, stay away from hairy, purple-leafed vines!"

Sultan let Petite lead after that. The pony had a better idea of which plants to stay away from! Before long, the trees were fewer and not as tall. Eventually, the woods lay behind them.

"We made it!" Sultan said. He unrolled the map. Dreamy planted herself on the edge to keep it flat. Sultan traced his paw over the route. "There's the mountain.

There are the woods." He tapped a spot on the map. "And here's the wall." Sultan looked up. "Straight ahead."

The pets tramped onward. Sometimes Sultan led the way. Sometimes Treasure or Pumpkin did. Being first or fastest didn't matter as much to Sultan. In the end, he just cared about getting there.

Berry kept stopping to pick berries. She popped a green one in her mouth. "Yum," she said. "Pickleberries! They're hard to find!"

Sultan and Dreamy walked side by side.

"I hope you find your ball," Dreamy said.

"I'm sorry I asked if you should stay home," Sultan said. "You've helped so much! First the map, then the vine—"

"That's okay," Dreamy said. "We're different. You like to run. I like to nap. But sometimes different pets make good friends."

"Definitely," Sultan said with a happy growl.

Dreamy nudged Sultan with her shoulder. She pointed a paw in front of her. "Is that a wall?" she asked.

Sultan narrowed his eyes. "Yes!" he cried.

Through the trees, he could just make out a high brick wall. It reminded him of the wall behind Lucy's shop.

But it couldn't be. Not after all the land they'd crossed.

He took off running. When he got to the wall, he launched himself at it and landed about halfway up. But his claws found nothing to grip. He slid back down.

"That didn't work," Pumpkin said.

"We need a better way," Petite said.

"I bet you could climb that tree," Dreamy said. The kitten pointed to a tree near the wall. "Or jump to one of its branches, then to the top of the wall."

Sultan swished his tail. Once again,

he was glad Dreamy had come along. And not just because she'd had another good idea. It was because she was a good friend.

Sultan went first but waited at the top of the tree to make sure his friends could get to the wall safely. For once, he didn't mind the delay. Some things, like a special ball and good friends, were worth waiting for. Treasure and Dreamy used their claws to climb the tree, then hopped to the wall. Petite, Berry, and Pumpkin leaped to the branch, then to the wall.

Finally, Sultan scrambled from the tree to the wall and looked out over the other side.

The wall enclosed a beautiful garden of soft green grass. Peach, pear, and apple trees lined the edges. Roses, lilies, and sunflowers were planted thickly between the trunks.

Sultan scanned the garden. What about the ball? Where was it?

A glimmer of light caught his eye. There! In the middle of the garden was a beautiful ball, resting on a marble pedestal. It wasn't golden. It was a deep, rich, midnight blue, with bright blue paw prints, just like the ball at Lucy's shop.

Sultan's heart leaped. This ball gave him the same feeling he'd had in the snake's cave.

This ball was *magical*!

Sultan jumped to the ground. He padded over to the pedestal. He rolled up on his back legs and touched the shiny ball with both paws. It felt cool and warm at the same time. He rubbed his cheek against it and purred.

Behind him, the pets cheered. Petite whinnied. Berry thumped her foot.

"It's a dream come true," Dreamy said happily.

With his claws tucked in, Sultan pulled the ball, *his* ball, toward him. "I'm so glad Lucy told me about this ball," he said.

"You know, I was thinking the brick wall reminded me of somewhere," Treasure said. "It looks like the wall at the back of the Squeak and Ball Supply Shop!"

"That Lucy is good," Berry said. "She knows exactly what makes her customers happy."

Just then, a door opened at the far end

of the garden. Lucy trotted out with a big smile on her face. "You found it!" she said.

Sultan nodded. He wasn't surprised to see her.

"Did you enjoy the adventure?" Lucy asked.

"Yes," Sultan said. "I know it's the same ball you showed me before. But working hard for it makes it special."

"You're wise, Sultan," Lucy said, "as well as brave."

Berry giggled. "Tell us the story about how you found *this* ball," she said to Sultan.

"Yes, tell us!" Lucy chimed in. "I want to hear."

Sultan raised himself up. The pets and Lucy settled around him. Dreamy closed her eyes, but Sultan knew she was listening.

"First we faced a mountain," he said. "Then the woods. Then a high wall. Luckily, I had friends to help me. I couldn't have done it alone."

"That's us!" Pumpkin said, her tail wagging. "We're in the story!"

"Climbing the mountain, we almost got caught in a rockslide!" Sultan went on.

"And I lost the map. But luckily Dreamy saved it."

Dreamy opened her eyes. She winked at Sultan. He winked back.

"In the woods, a strangler vine grabbed

me!" Sultan said, shivering. "But my friends came to the rescue!"

Pumpkin, Petite, Treasure, Lucy, and Berry listened, their eyes wide. No one blinked.

"Then there was the wall. It was super high. But we found a way over it!"

Berry rocked back on her heels. "We did!"

Sultan leaned forward. The other pets leaned toward him. "In the end, I didn't just find my ball. I found out a secret, too." Sultan paused. "Adventures are more fun with friends."

"It's true," Lucy said. Pumpkin and Petite nodded.

"I like adventures!" Berry announced.

"When can we have another?" asked Treasure.

Dreamy smiled in her sleep.

Another adventure? Sultan's whiskers twitched. He was ready—any time!

He rested his chin on the beautiful midnight-blue ball. He would have so much fun playing with it in the jungle gym!

But first he had to scale a wall, cross

the woods, and climb a mountain with his friends . . . again!

Sure, it was faster to take a gently sloping cobblestone path home. But where was the adventure in that?